Change

Dyslexic Friendly Edition

A Message

by

Evelyn Rainey

First presented at United Methodist Temple, Lakeland, FL April 28, 2024.

ISBN-13: 978-1-963272-11-6

ShelteringTree.Earth, LLC

PO Box 973, Eagle Lake, FL 33839

ShelteringTreeMedia.com

What is a "Dyslexic Friendly" Book?

Sheltering Tree Media has taken steps to make our books more friendly for those who live with dyslexia. While the following principles will not make every book readable for every reader, it is our best effort to create products that encourage reading and to support all readers.

Throughout the book, we use a font named OpenDyslexic. This is a free font that is designed to help dyslexic readers distinguish each letter from the others. For more information about OpenDyslexic, how it differs from other fonts, and research behind the font, visit their website: www.opendyslexic.com.

In our books created for adults, we use 12-point font. This size font provides the reader with plenty of spacing between the letters (which is called *kerning*). The bigger, wider font tends to be easier to the reader's eyes.

The space between each word is increased (this is called *word spacing*). This helps better to distinguish when one word ends and the next begins. The line spacing is greater than most common fonts (this is called *leading*). This all should help with readability.

Whenever possible, the text is Left-Aligned but it is not justified on the right side. Allowing the right side of a paragraph to remain *rough* keeps the word spacing consistent throughout.

Our Dyslexic Friendly books are printed on cream or ivory paper which is also thicker than the average book page. This minimizes the sharp contrast of black-on-white pages as well as bleed-through of text from the previous page.

Finally, Sheltering Tree Media has made colored overlays available when you purchase a book through our online store. You can find these overlays at ShelteringTreeMedia.com/shop/dyslexic-friendly.

These are some of the principles we use to create a book as readable as possible to those living with dyslexia. Some may find this helpful; some may not. Please provide us with any insights you might have to improve our Dyslexic Friendly principles. We pray this will enable many to heighten their love for reading.

DEDICATION

For all those who saw the image
and likeness of God within me and
helped me along the path which God
has set before me.

Pastoral Prayer

Dearest God, Utmost Divine, Holy Spirit, and Jesus the Christ,

We come today to praise your name and worship at your feet.

We ask you, Lord, to give us what we need: food, shelter, belonging, loved ones, and most importantly, a purpose in your kingdom. We ask for peace within our souls as we stand in a world of war. We ask for the ability to confer understanding in a world divided by deceit and betrayal. We ask for empathy in a world filled with apathy.

And we ask that You forgive us for the things we have done which were wrong. We ask you to forgive us for the things we did not do which we should have done. We ask you to forgive us for being cowards when you have shown us how to live courageously without fear.

1

In turn, let us forgive those who have abused us, those who have betrayed us, those who have hurt us intentionally or unintentionally. We especially want to forgive those who just ignored us, as if we were not worthy of attention.

We ask for strength to face what is to come. To stand against the foe and fight for what is true and right. We know that the victory is yours – earned by your sacrifice and enjoyed by all who call on your name.

We ask especially that we learn how to align ourselves with you when all that we know and love and depend on changes. You do not change.

And now, together as the body and bride of Christ, we repeat the prayer you taught us:

Our Father, which art in heaven, hollowed be your name.

Thy kingdom come; thy will be done On Earth as it is in heaven.

Give us this day our daily bread.

And forgive us our sins as we forgive those who sin against us.

And lead us not into temptation.

But deliver us from evil.

For thine is the kingdom, and the power, and the glory, forever.

Amen.

Introduction

I'm Evelyn Rainey, and I am honored to share with you this morning in Pastor Pam's absence. You know me for who I am to this church: I facilitate a prayer shawl ministry. I organize the ushers and greeters every three months. (If I haven't called you yet, I will. I promise!) I lead the team which organizes and runs the Senior Adult Game Days. I'm on the Pastor-Parish Relationship Council. I've been the liturgist several times and hope to do so again. I've sung a few solos and plan to join the choir once my Wednesday nights are free. And I am in the process of becoming a minister in the United Methodist Church.

But that may be all you know about me.

So, I am the daughter of the late Major Robert Kendrick Rainey and Marion Presley Rainey. I am my mother's legal guardian and full-time caregiver as she travels the final journey on this Earth. I was raised in churches wherever we were stationed around the world as my mother led the children's choirs and played the piano or organ and my father taught Sunday School classes. I was raised to believe that one does not just go to church, sit and listen, and then get up and leave. To belong to a church means to work for the kingdom of God.

I am also a sister, a cousin, an aunt, a mother, and a grandmother.

I spent 38 years teaching various grades and classes in public schools. I thank God for every single day - of my retirement!

I'm a published author and have been a guest author or speaker in conventions, conferences, and workshops across the southeast United States. I love that so much that I started my own publishing company which has expanded into a media company. Our motto is: We publish books to help you feed His sheep.

And, my dear friends, know this: I'm not a stranger to sorrow. I'm not a stranger to trauma. I'm not a stranger to life-shattering disasters. And neither are you.

But I'm not a stranger to Joy, either. I chose joy as my focus. And I hope you do, too.

Our Scripture today comes from Romans 8:38-39[1]

[38] For I am persuaded that neither death nor life, nor angels nor rulers, nor things present nor things to come, nor powers, [39] nor height nor depth, nor any other created thing will be able to separate us from the love of God that is in Christ Jesus our Lord.

Father, Here I stand as your vessel. Fill me with your Holy Spirit and let the words that pour out of my lips be yours. Let them touch the hearts and minds of those who need to hear them. Amen.

The Message

Change.

Things Change, and we don't like that.

You would think that – as much as everything we know changes, that we would be used to the idea that – things change.

But we're not happy. We don't want things to change. We don't like it when things change. Even if it's a good change, we are often resistant to the change, just because it's change!

I'd like you to think about the things that cause changes in your life.

One of the most obvious changes this month here at UMT is – most of the winter visitors have gone back up north, so our pews are abundantly empty. But you and I are still here. And those of you viewing us on Facebook and YouTube are still here – or there!

What else causes major life changes?

Disease.
Covid is the disease which will define our generation. It changed our ability to meet in churches, groups, schools, and shops. For two years, we feared hugging someone. And that fear lingers even today. According to the World Health Organization, over 15 million people died from the coronavirus within the first two years. But there have been pandemics before and will be again.

Disease is a very powerful change agent.

Weather causes changes. Floridians dread the first of June because it indicates the beginning of hurricane season and all the changes that a bad storm can present. The first snow can change the landscape. Fog can change the way you drive. Other weather-based changes include tornadoes and tsunamis.

I'm sure you've heard the adage, "**Politics** makes strange bedfellows." Politics can swing a country left or it can swing the country right. It can plow through old mindsets - or build new walls. Politics is a change agent, whether you live in a democracy, theocrasy, dictatorship, or total anarchy.

We heard from Cuban ministers over the last two Sundays about the horrific living conditions in communist Cuba.

We are delighted to learn that Cuba is changing back to a more civilized country. We thank God that attempts of the communist leaders to crush Christianity **were not successful**, not only in Cuba but across the world.

But we must never forget, we humans are at the mercy of political change.

Changes also come from the simple truth of growing old. In John 21:18 Jesus said,

> "Truly, truly I tell you, when you were younger, you used to put on your belt and walk wherever you wanted; but when you grow old, you will stretch out your hands and someone else will put your belt on you and bring you where you do not want to go."

Change is not necessarily BAD. There are good changes, too. We have all experienced good and bad **major life changes:** accidents – providential or destructive, the death of a loved one – sudden and cruel, or merciful and long-awaited. The birth or adoption of a new child or grandchild, the beginning of a relationship or the end of one.

The way the world is today has changed from the way it was when I was a child, and the way the world may be tomorrow will change – for better or for worse - with or without our consent.

Everything that is a part of our human existence changes!

Everything changes! We know that things change!

Why does that upset us so?

Genesis 1:26 says that God made us in His image and likeness and gave us authority over all the mammals, fish, birds, and reptiles.

I believe this – that we are made in the image and likeness of God and that we have control over all other living things. Shouldn't this being the *image and likeness of God* set us apart from all these changes?

Malachi 3:6 says, "Because I, the LORD, have not changed, you descendants of Jacob have not been destroyed."

And Numbers 23:19 states, "God is not a man, that he might lie, or a son of man, that he might change his mind.

God does not change!

So, could it be that the spark of God within us, that which is the image and likeness of God yearns for the changelessness of God?

When you yearn for something, you feel hollow, empty, unfulfilled and these emotions lead you to feel anxious. Synonyms for yearn are hunger and thirst. The same pair of words Jesus used to describe as Blessed:

Blessed are those who hunger and thirst for righteousness, for they will be filled. (Matthew 5:6). In Matthew 25:35, Jesus said, "³⁵ "'For I was hungry, and you gave me something to eat; I was thirsty and you gave me something to drink."

Hunger and Thirst – to Yearn

Do you yearn for the changelessness of God? Because you are made in the image and likeness of God, do you yearn to be as unchanging as God?

When changes happen, **we hunger and thirst for changelessness.**

So, when things change, and you know they are going to, **how do you connect that holy spark of the image and likeness of God within you to the God who does not change?**

Romans 8:38-39 reminds us of things that change, but promises that none of these **things that change** can separate us from God:

    ³⁸ For I am persuaded that neither death nor life,
    nor angels nor rulers,
    nor things present nor things to come,
    nor powers,
    ³⁹ nor height nor depth,
    nor any other created thing – **or may I interject here – nor anything that CHANGES –**
    will be able to separate us from the love of God that is in Christ Jesus our Lord.

But Paul did not tell us **HOW** to keep aligned with God **when things change.**

When things change, whether you want them to change or not, you feel like your whole world has been tossed to-and-fro, like a ship on a stormy sea.

Like a ship on a storm-tossed sea, you are always going to be at the mercy of changes.

Acts 27:29 says, "Then, fearing we might run aground on the rocks, they dropped four anchors from the stern and prayed for daylight to come."

Four anchors! One anchor before them at the **bow**, one behind them at the **stern**, one to the left side on the **port** and one to the right side on the **starboard**. These anchors held the ship in alignment with the Earth, despite the battering waves and twisting winds.

A great number of our members were in the Navy, so you know -- Sailors know how to align their ships during changes caused by storms.

So, how do we align ourselves with God during change?

Matthew 6:33 reads, "But seek first *the kingdom of God and His righteousness, and all these things will be provided for you.*"

Seek God.
Become aligned with God.
Anchor yourself to God.
And don't be afraid of the storm.

Do you have some storms in your life right now? Lord knows, I do.

So how does one seek God and successfully find Him?

John Wesley called these ways of seeking and finding God **Acts of Piety** and **Acts of Mercy.**

The Acts of Piety are the first three anchors: Prayer, Praise, and Worship.

Prayer – that's the anchor that you place at the bow of your ship. Your prayers go before you in all things.

First Thessalonians 5:17 states, "*Pray without ceasing.*"

When you hear an ambulance, pray, "Lord, guard and guide."
When you hear of someone in harm's way, pray, "Lord, protect and preserve."
When someone you love – or hate - is going through a difficult time, pray, "Lord, direct and defend."

Pray before meals, pray before bed, pray when you first open your eyes. So, **BEFORE** the storms of change rage, place prayer at the bow of your ship, **to go before you in all things that change.**

Praise – that's the anchor that you place to the portside. Praise is your gift to God. Psalm 150 begins with:

> [1] *Praise the LORD!*
> *Praise God in His sanctuary;*
> *Praise Him in His mighty expanse.*
> [2] *Praise Him for His mighty deeds;*
> *Praise Him according to His excellent greatness.*

2 Corinthians 12:10 even says to praise God for your persecutions:

> *Therefore I delight in weaknesses, in insults, in distresses, in persecutions, in difficulties, in behalf of Christ; for when I am weak, then I am strong.*

So, every time the storms of change rage, and you lift your left hand to work or in joy or in anger or in protest against those changes, **praise God.** Use your praises to **anchor yourself** to Him.

Worship is the anchor you place at your starboard side. Worship is your relationship with God.

You can worship **personally and privately** through meditation, reading the Bible, and living a clean life.

You can worship **publicly** through singing hymns, reciting creeds and Scriptures, attending worship services in person or online.

You can worship through **sacred rituals and sacraments** such as Holy Communion and Baptism.

You can worship through music, dance, art, and writing.

So, every time the storms of change rage, **anchor yourself** through **worship** to God.

Prayer is the anchor you set in front of you. Praise is the anchor you set on your left. Worship is the anchor you set at your right. These three anchors will hold you through most changes. But you must place one more – and this is the anchor you leave behind you – your **Acts of Mercy.**

Jesus said, [35] "For I was hungry and you gave me something to eat; I was thirsty and you gave me something to drink; I was a stranger and you took me in; [36] I was naked and you clothed me; I was sick and you took care of me; I was in prison and you visited me."

How do you feed the hungry?

I'm not talking about UMT now; I'm talking about you personally. How do **you** feed the hungry?

Not just those who hunger for food but those who hunger for belonging and love.

How do you feed them?

How do you slake the thirst of those around you?

Do you help build a clean water well in an undeveloped country?

Do you smile at someone whose life has dried up with loneliness?

How do you slake their thirst?

How do you treat strangers?

Do you welcome them into your community, into your house, into your church, even if they look different than you do, or eat differently, or love differently?

Do you remember that **they, too,** are made in the image and likeness of God?

For those whose sins and mistakes have been laid bare before the whole world, do you tell them that God forgives them?

Do you clothe them in **your** forgetfulness of what they did?

Do you help restore their self-respect?

How do you take care of the sick?

Do you write personal cards or make phone calls?

Do you drop a cake or a good book by?

Do you help them with the cost of their prescriptions?

Do you go over to their house and clean their kitchen and do a load of laundry?

And those who are imprisoned by sin,

imprisoned by abuse,

or imprisoned by fear, or depression, or despair –

Do you even see the bars which form their prison?

Do you recognize the signs that someone is imprisoned?

Do you tell them that, once they get out of prison *they sure will be welcomed* in church? Because that's a good thing to do! That gives them a future to look forward to and a fellowship of Christians to belong to.

But more than that, do you take them by the hand and stand beside them and remind them

- not that things will change –
because **things change** whether we want them to or not,

but do you remind them that they must *Seek First the Kingdom of God*, so that they can survive the battering waves and twisting winds until their storm is over and daylight comes.

If you do these Acts of Piety (Prayer, Praise, and Worship) and these Acts of Mercy (feeding the hungry, satisfying the thirsty, welcoming the stranger, clothing the naked, caring for the sick, and visiting those who are imprisoned), then all the things that change cannot separate you from the love of God, **because you will have anchored yourself to God, and God does not change.**

Benediction

As you leave this sanctuary,
this safe place of prayer, praise, and
worship, and go into the world to
perform your works of Mercy,
remember that:
    Christ is with you,
    Christ goes before you,
    Christ supports behind you,
    Christ is on your right,
    Christ is on your left,
    Christ will flow through you in
all that you do.
    Go in peace.

Resources, Scriptures, and Holy Writings

Matthew 25:35-36

[35] "For I was hungry and you gave me something to eat; I was thirsty and you gave me something to drink; I was a stranger and you took me in; [36] I was naked and you clothed me; I was sick and you took care of me; I was in prison and you visited me."

Genesis 1:26

Then God said, "Let us make man in our **image**, according to our **likeness**. They will rule the fish of the sea, the birds of the sky, the livestock that roam the whole earth, **and** the creatures that crawl on the earth."

Romans 8:38-39

[38] For I am persuaded that neither death nor life, nor angels nor rulers, nor things present nor things to come, nor powers, [39] nor height nor depth, nor any other created thing will be able to separate us from the love of God that is in Christ Jesus our Lord.

Matthew 6:33

But **seek first the kingdom of God** and his righteousness, and all these things will be provided for you.

John 21:18

Truly, truly I tell you, when you were younger, you used to put on your belt and walk wherever you wanted; but when you grow old, you will stretch out your hands and someone else will put your belt on you, and bring you where you do not want to go."

St. Teresa of Avila[2]

Let nothing disturb thee,
Nothing affright thee;
All things are passing,
God never changeth!
Patient endurance attaineth to all things;
Who God possesseth in nothing is wanting;
Alone God sufficeth.

Hymns:[3]

Preparatory: *Great is Thy Faithfulness* (Words by Thomas O. Chisholm, 1923 based on Lamentations 3:22-23; Music by William M. Runyan, 1923) #140

Conclusion: *Seek ye First the Kingdom of God* (Words and Music by Karen Lafferty, 1972) #405

Notes

[1] The Scriptures used through this message come from The Christian Standard Bible. Copyright © 2017 by Holman Bible Publishers. You may of course use any version of the Bible as you see fit.

[2] *The Song Book of the Salvation Army* page 956, translated by Henry Wadsworth Longfellow

[3] *The United Methodist Hymnal*, United Methodist Publishing House: Nashville, 1989 (the Red Hymnal)

ABOUT THE AUTHOR

Evelyn Rainey has always loved to tell stories and help others understand. As such, she is a published author and educator. But she is also the caregiver of her mother, an herb and vegetable gardener, cat wrangler, and crochet artist. She manages **ShelteringTree.Earth, LLC Publishing** and facilitates the **United Methodist Temple** Prayer Shawl

Ministry and the Senior Adults Program there, as well as serving on the SPRC. She facilitates an online support group for parents who have adult or juvenile children in jails and prisons (Parents of Prosecuted Children Support Group POPCSupport.com) She is in the process of becoming a Licensed Local Pastor through the United Methodist Church.

After 38 years in education, Evelyn retired after having earned BS degrees and Certificates of Endorsement in Early Childhood Education, Elementary Education, Gifted Education, Integrated Middle School Curriculum, English for Speakers of Other Languages, and Journalism. She also taught all grade levels from Kindergarten through Adult and at many different facilities, including jails and teen pregnancy centers.

Evelyn has over a dozen books published including science fiction, fantasy, historical fiction, new age urban fantasy, metaphysical and visionary, pastoral handbooks, and children's books. She has facilitated writer groups (and continues to do so with on-line meetings. If you would like to join one, you would be very welcome. See https://www.shelteringtreemedia.com/events). She has been guest speaker and guest author at writer conferences and conventions throughout the southeast US.

Her love of teaching has expanded into videos for book trailers, crochet lessons, meditation series, Bible studies, as well as interviews and writing lessons. (See her YouTube channel **evelynrainey4780**.)

Unable to travel as long as she remains her mother's caregiver, Evelyn is still able to conduct interviews and conferences via phone and video communication. She welcomes questions and comments from her readers but prefers to be contacted initially through https://evelynrainey.com/contact.

DISCUSSION GUIDE FOR CLASSES, JOURNALING, OR PERSONAL CONTEMPLATION

Discuss &/or write your answers.

1. Name three good changes that you have experienced. Why were they good?

_____

_____

_____

_____

2. Name three bad changes that you have experienced. Why were they bad?

_____

_____

_____

_____

3. Describe a time in your life when you didn't want anything to change.

_____

_____

_____

_____

4. Describe a time in your life when all you wanted was for things to change.

_____

_____

_____

_____

5. Do you agree or disagree that God does not change? Support your answer by evidence other than the Scriptures.

_____

_____

_____

_____

6. In your own words, define Acts of Piety.

_____

_____

_____

_____

7. Which Act of Piety – prayer, praise, or worship – do you think is most important? Why?

_____

_____

_____

_____

8. In what ways has prayer changed through history?

_____

_____

_____

_____

9. In what ways has praise changed through history?

_____

_____

_____

_____

10. In what ways has worship changed through history?

_____

_____

_____

_____

11. How have these Acts of Piety changed through your Christian life?

_____

_____

_____

_____

12. Do you think that Jesus stated the Acts of Mercy in a specific order? If so, what was that order and why?

_____

_____

_____

_____

13. Rank the Acts of Mercy by their importance to you - one being the most important, five being the least. Explain your reasoning.

_____ feeding the sick

_____ giving water to the thirsty

_____ welcoming the stranger

_____ clothing the naked

_____ taking care of the sick

_____ visiting the imprisoned

_____

_____

_____

_____

_____

_____

_____

14. Rank the Acts of Mercy by how easy they are for you to do - one being the easiest, five being the most difficult. Explain your reasoning.

_____ feeding the sick

_____ giving water to the thirsty

_____ welcoming the stranger

_____ clothing the naked

_____ taking care of the sick

_____ visiting the imprisoned

15. Rank the Acts of Mercy by how well your church does these things - one being the best and most often done, five being the worst or least often done. Explain your reasoning.

_____ feeding the sick

_____ giving water to the thirsty

_____ welcoming the stranger

_____ clothing the naked

_____ taking care of the sick

_____ visiting the imprisoned

16. Look at the Acts of Piety that you do the best. Develop a plan to help others implement these in their own lives.

17. Look at the Acts of Piety that you do the least well. Develop a plan to help yourself improve these in your life.

18. Look at the Acts of Mercy that you do the best. Develop a plan to help others implement these in their own lives.

19. Look at the Acts of Mercy that you do the least well. Develop a plan to help yourself improve these in your life.

20. What have you learned through this message?

SHELTERING TREE

Earth
Publishing

ShelteringTreeMedia.com

For more information,
to become one of our authors, translators,
or illustrators, or to contact the author:

ShelteringTreeMedia.com

www.ingramcontent.com/pod-product-compliance
Lightning Source LLC
Chambersburg PA
CBHW031903170626
46807CB00004B/1874